HOW TO HANDLE DOMESTIC VIOLENCE

SOLUTION AT LAST

Oluwatoyin Babatunde

How To Handle Domestic Violence
Copyright © 2020 by Oluwatoyin Babatunde

Published by **Janrick Publishing**
West Yorkshire, U.K.

ISBN - 9798687001984 (pbk)

DEDICATION

I dedicate this book to the Almighty God my maker.

The God of Abraham, Isaac and Jacob.

The Alpha and the Omega.

Creator of the heaven of the earth.

The one who instigated the writing of this book.

To Him alone be all the glory and honour.

ACKNOWLEDGEMENT

First and foremost, I want to show gratitude to the Almighty God, who inspired the writing of this book. The great I am that I am. The one who is my salvation, my strength, my wisdom, the lifter up of my head and the hope of my glory. It's not by man's wisdom, but to Him alone be all the glory.

I want to appreciate my husband, my best friend, my number one fan, my Pastor, prayer partner and confidant, who is the first proof-reader of the book. Thanks for your support at all times. Thanks for allowing me to be me. He sometimes allowed me to stay behind alone at night, while he'd gone to bed, so I could have time to complete the writing of the book. Thank you and love you loads.

I am grateful to God for giving me a unique father in my father in the Lord, Bishop Taiwo V. Adelakun. He is not only my Spiritual father, but took up the role of my biological father, since dad's demise. You are a great role model sir. Thanks for always teaching us to live a life that will be pleasing to God. You are a great vessel of honour in the hands of God to raise armies of victorious and prosperous saints for Him. Thank you for allowing God use you to make my husband and I discover God's calling on our lives sir. I am grateful sir.

I am eternally grateful to my mother in the Lord, Pastor Dolapo Adelakun, who despite her busy schedule, was able to forward this book. I was so much looking forward to your comments on the book, because I know that you will not hide your honest thought about the book. I deeply appreciate you mum. Thanks for your motherly care and love, your mentoring, teachings, encouragement, love and large heart. Your passion to share the gift of your time and wisdom to develop future leaders is non- comparable ma. I found a great role model in you ma, which has really helped me in the journey of life. I wonder how I would have coped in ministry if God had not made our paths cross. Thank you for being there always mum. This writing grace was inherited from you mum. I'm so grateful.

My appreciation also goes to Dr Mrs Oludotun Ologunebi, my amiable partner in the work of the kingdom, sister from another mother, who took time to proofread the book. Thank you to my proof-reader, Sister Janice Pinard. I appreciate you, and thank you for believing in me since our paths crossed. Thank you for your support always. Pst D, my sister from another mother, I appreciate you.

I also want to thank God for my children, Esther, Fisayomi and Samuel Babatunde. You gave me the peace of mind to be able to carry out my role as a mother and still be able to function in my God given assignment. You are so special to me. Thanks for your support, love and care at all times.

I cannot do without appreciating all my sisters, brothers and children at Victory International Church, North London. Thanks for your support at all times. You are all loving, wonderful and amazing. It's a privilege having you around us. Thank you loads.

My appreciation also goes to my biological sisters and brothers. Yemi Adediran, Jide Adegoke, Folake Araoye, Ademola Adegoke and Bola Ajijola. You are wonderful siblings. I couldn't have asked God for better siblings.

I appreciate God for all my extended families, especially my uncles, my wonderful and amazing In-laws, friends, all our friends and families on MARITAL MATTERS and all VIC Pastors.

Lastly, I want to appreciate my biological parents, who have gone to be with the Lord. Rev James Sunday Adegoke and Evangelist Emily Adegoke. Thank you for bringing me up in the way of the Lord. Your labour is not in vain. Rest on, till we meet to part no more.

PREFACE

I have always wondered how and why a human being can be brutal to a fellow human being. Especially the one they are meant to love and be intimate with. Intimacy with a spouse should always bring a smile to the face of both parties and the people around them, but that has not been the experience of some. Recent reports in the media have revealed an increase in incidents of domestic violence and this has led me to wonder what the cause could be. Despite the efforts of the government to eradicate or reduce the incidents, they seem to be increasing, with resultant human casualties. My vocation as a Minister of religion (Pastor), exposed me to a few cases of domestic violence. In many of these cases that I've witnessed, when all the issues have been looked into, there has been no justification for anyone to be brutal to their spouse and there would never be. No matter the provocation, resorting to violence can never be a solution.

During the Corona Virus lockdown, it was reported by the police that domestic violence incidents rose by one hundred percent. This statistic saddened and also angered me as I felt empathy for the victims. I was ready to write my blunt opinion about the culprits in expressing my anger on my Facebook platform, but my intention was interrupted by the Holy Spirit who revealed to me that there is more to violent behaviour in the home than meets the eye. Writing on Facebook will not change them. Although I had done a program on domestic violence before, I had no intention of writing about it yet because I have some other books lined up for writing. However, the creator interrupted my plan and inspired me to write His mind about domestic violence because He was ready to put a perpetual end to the damaging works of domestic violence. He decided to use this book to bring a smile to the faces of those who have suffered domestic violence in the hands of their supposed lover man/lover woman; to heal the perpetrators of their uncontrollable anger; to stop history being repeated in their children's lives; and to restore peace and purpose to their home. "I will use the most stupid things of the world to confound the wise," says the Lord.

The Holy Spirit made me realise that putting the perpetrators in jail cannot stop them from being violent, but rather cause their subsequent spouse to suffer even more violence. He revealed to me that there is always a root cause of their violent behaviour and until the root is dealt with, there can never be a permanent solution to their violent problem. Every other measure applied will only deal with the fruit, but the root will spring up again to bring forth violent fruits. That is why a man beats his wife, comes back to his senses to apologise but then does it again. The behaviour is rooted in them and needs to be uprooted. God is not happy with the effect of domestic violence on the victims, the affected spouse and children brought up in that environment, hence, bringing about this solution. It was an eye-opener and I'm very convinced that this revelation will bring healing to many homes who come in contact with this book and are ready to do what is written by the inspiration of the Holy Spirit. This solution strategy has been tried and tested, testimony abounds. It's your turn to share your testimony of God's goodness.

Contents

Foreword by Pastor Mrs Dolapo Adelakun

This book is a ready textbook for marriage counsellors. It is a complete healing dose. Very detailed, touching and fairly addressing all parties involved..... from the culprit to the victim to the offsprings.

Written in a gentle and captivating tone, its magnetic touch leaves you reading through without dropping it.

One thing that stuck with me in the book is that violence is the spirit of the beast. God never wants man to behave like a beast because he is created in God's image and likeness. I got this!

It's a book recommended for those who have a following and desire Peace for the marriages of their followers.

Couples need to read this. It's an eye-opener to check and possibly put an end to domestic violence. Our young ladies also should be armed with the information in this write-up.

The presentation is healthy and well balanced without any iota of condemnation or self-righteousness. It is a diet well served and free of poison.

The narrative is both educative and proactive. Soothing and refreshing. Spiced with relevant scriptures to inform and reform.

I pray this write up will bring healing and deliverance to many beautiful marriages the devil has marked for extinction.

Pastor Toyin, thank you for adding your voice to this generation. Thank you for sharing in the pain of so many couples who are reeling under the scars of abuse.

May this book accomplish the purpose for which it is written. May the Spirit of God breathe upon it to fulfil the healing it is meant for.

May the Lord give it wings to get to places you might never set your feet on.

This will not be your last write up. Jehovah will bring out all he has conceived in you. There shall be no abortion of gifts.

Happy Reading..... Get it across to couples all over and together we shall bring healing to our world.

Pastor Dolapo Adelakun

Dolapo Adelakun Mentoring Ministry

Aka Damsel.

Introduction

They both walk down the aisle with glittering smiley faces. She never wished for anything better than the kind of man she walked down the aisle with. Unknown to her, that the excitement would last for less than two weeks, after which the true nature of her wonderful dream spouse will become apparent and evolve into a hammer-like monster that hits so hard to scare and damage her mind. She was to discover that her marriage could condemn her to live a life of uncertainty and endangerment - every moment she spent in that relationship. Before long, the smiley face had become a long, teary and sorrowful one, as the hope of a loving, caring, reasonable, life partner had slipped away. This was all due to the sudden personality change of the once loving spouse who now decks her face with blows at every opportunity, even without provocation. Amazingly, her love for her spouse was so strong that even the battering could not dissolve it. The last thing she wanted was to be away from her spouse, even for a day. Her dream was to cling to her spouse, according to the vow she made on that exalted alter, before her maker - in sickness, in health, in riches, in poverty in any situation, until death do they part. She couldn't imagine any situation that could put them apart. But this new development and escalating violence is a threat to her dream, which she could not contemplate abandoning not even under the present circumstances. Although she is scared of the danger and risk of continually living with an abusive spouse, she could not contemplate ending her marriage.

As she continued to hide the unpleasant tone of her marriage, a similar scenario was being played out in her elder sister's home, where her own marriage of 4 years, was turning into a theatre of war. Both sisters kept their marital troubles away from the scrutiny of their families. Although she had been curious on occasions when the sister had shown up with bruised cheek or scratched nose with the excuse of running into the toilet door, it didn't occur to her that the bruises could be related to fisticuffs with her spouse.

Does the above sound familiar to you?

Domestic Violence

According to the Office of National Statistics (ONS) about 4.2% of men and 7.9% of women suffered domestic abuse in England and Wales during 2018. This equates to about 685,000 male victims and 1,300,000 women. Murders related to domestic violence are at a five year high. The majority of victims are women and the majority of suspects are men. In 2019, 173 people were killed in domestic violence-related homicides, according to data obtained by the BBC from 43 police forces across the United Kingdom.

These statistics are so alarming that the government had to put legislation in place to guide how to handle such behaviour. They are doing the best they know to do in an effort to use the criminal justice system to curtail the incidents of fatalities in domestic violence. The government has committed so much resources to protect the victims of domestic violence. However, all these measures are temporary, because there have been cases where the abusive spouse was prepared to menacingly lurk in the shadows in a predatory manner and then viciously hunt down their victims who are supposed to be under the protection of the state. Sometimes, the children from the marriage are not spared the murderous carnage that often concludes such sad relationships. This indicates that a solution has not been found to this deadly situation.

There is however, good news to the readers of this book. Finally, there is an absolute and permanent solution to your fear. You might have read so many books or heard so much advice that divorce is the answer or solution to domestic violence. Whereas, this is not what you have wished for. Your long awaited solution is here, as this book reveals how you can bring a long-lasting solution to the domestic violence you have been experiencing. You will have no fear of the culprit coming back to haunt you again and your desire of having a violent free home will be fulfilled. This book will address how your children who have been under the risk of emotional and psychological damage can find permanent healing and a change of perception. This book will also address how the smile you had on your face on the day both of you walk down the aisle can return again, and how your dream of a long-lasting relationship (until death do you part) can be fulfilled. This book will also reveal to you, how the root of domestic violence, which is the main cause of the problem, can be handled. You will also have the opportunity to use prayer points in this book to wage war against that monster, called domestic violence.

My name is Oluwatoyin Babatunde, an associate Pastor at Victory International Church, North London. I am married to Pastor Michael Babatunde, Resident Pastor of Victory International Church, North London and together, we have three lovely children.

Nothing else qualified me to write this book because men are limited in knowledge. However, the grace of God has exposed me to this divine revelation from the creator of the heaven and the earth, who has answers to all questions and the strategies and power to change things. Although, to the glory of God, I have never experienced domestic violence, my qualifications for writing this insight and solution to domestic violence is divinely inspired. If I was relying on personal experience, I would have only been able to write or provide advice based on my experience, which will be limited to my own peculiarity. But my inspiration transpires beyond my knowledge and the wisdom of man. Even though I have had the chance to counsel and intervene in some domestic violence cases in my role as a pastor, the experience would still be inadequate and not qualify me to write this. So, I am writing this book from the position of a messenger who the mind of God, the creator of the institution of marriage, has benevolently chosen to use as a vessel, to reveal the insight to. To Him alone be all the glory, who created the heaven and the earth.

Be expectant and open up your mind to the content of this book, because the last domestic abuse you experienced from your spouse will be the last you will ever experience.

Background Of God's Will For Your Home.

God is a God of purpose. His reason for creating man and woman is with the intention for both of them becoming one. Mark 10:6-9 says, "For this cause shall a man leave his father and mother, and cleave to his wife; and they twain shall be one flesh: so then they are no more twain, but one flesh. What therefore God hath joined together, let not man put asunder."

Companionship is one of the reasons God instituted marriage, Genesis 2:18, "And the Lord God said, It is not good that the man should be alone; I will make him an help meet for him." Companionship progresses to having children, which is also one of the reasons God initiated marriage. If a couple's companionship is healthy, they will have happy and Godly children. If the companionship is toxic, if it is turbulent, the seed of the union will be unhappy and they might not turn out the way God wants them to, unless God intervenes. Malachi 2:15 says, "And did not he make one? Yet had he the residue of the spirit. And wherefore one? That he might seek a godly seed. Therefore, take heed to your spirit, and let none deal treacherously against the wife of his youth."

The fact that the devil knows God is interested in the peace and unity of your marriage is enough to make him throw weapons of disagreement and strife against your home. If you give him the chance, he'll destroy that union. The devil knows that there is power in your unity as a couple, and that the strength of your unity determines your blessings. A major weapon Satan uses to destroy marriages is domestic violence. It goes without saying that the purpose of the devil is being carried out when a marriage that is meant to bring joy has resulted in beatings and violence. That is why you must be sensitive to know that the devil is at work against your home, particularly when you notice anything contrary to the peace of God. The plan of God for husband and wife is to live in peace and unity. The Bible says for two shall become one. Living in peace and unity will allow the purpose of God concerning your home to come to pass. Knowing the will of God concerning your marriage makes you recognise when the enemy is at work. But many do not know that the enemy is at work, hence they start fighting the wrong person and giving strength to the enemy. The enemy of peace in your home is the devil, not your spouse. Both of you must come together to fight the enemy out of your home, no matter in what forms it comes, or else, he will have his way. It may come in different ways, such as infidelity, domestic violence, sexually abusing children, alcoholism, drugs, gambling, controlling behaviour and so on. In whatever forms it comes, you must recognise that it is the devil's handiwork and start resisting it immediately.

2 Corinthians 10:4-5 states "For the weapons of our warfare are not carnal, but mighty through God to the pulling down of strong holds; Casting down imaginations, and every high thing that exalted itself against the knowledge of God, and bringing into captivity every thought to the obedience of Christ." When you begin to experience domestic violence in your home, know that there is a mountain you need to conquer with everything in you. It's a sign that the enemy has come to kill, steal and destroy. The plan of the devil is to make your spouse look like your enemy. Resist the provocation to hate, resist the devil and he shall flee from you.

How To Overcome Domestic Violence.

Domestic violence is a deadly virus that has led to many untimely deaths, permanent injury, as well as divorce which God specifically said He hates, according to Malachi 2:16.

It amazes me whenever I hear about domestic violence. On one particular occasion, I heard of the increased rate in domestic violence during general lockdown in societies caused by the dangers of Corona Virus infection. When I heard of the rising incidents of domestic abuse, I was about to express my anger, by writing my disappointment and disapproval on my Facebook wall. However, the Holy Spirit called me to order, and interrupted my perception. He made me to understand that there is more to their behaviour than meets the eye. There's a root to every act of violent behaviour. Writing to disapprove their behaviour will not change anything in them until the root cause of their behaviour is dealt with.

Only beasts of the field are brutal and fight for recognition in order to control other animals. Animals resort to brutal physical force to exert dominion over other animals in order to eat them or sometimes to display their physical superiority and be recognised as the king of the field. You can refer to an animal as a beast, especially if it is a large, dangerous, or unusual in size and ferocity. But when you refer to a man as a beast, you mean that his behaviour, especially his sexual behaviour and/or other behaviour is very violent and uncontrolled.

Domestic violence is defined as any pattern of incidents of controlling, coercive or threatening behaviour, violence or abuse, between those 16 or over who are or have been intimate partners or family members, regardless of their gender or sexuality. Domestic violence is not gender exclusive and can be perpetrated by either men or women. It can be described as Psychological, Physical, Sexual, Financial or Emotional. For the purpose of this book, I will be addressing mainly Physical Abuse.

God did not create us to be violent towards each other as human beings because we were created in His own image. It was when the devil found his way into the heart of men that men became violent towards one another. That is why you must handle the issue of domestic violence spiritually. God did not create human beings to be abusive. An animal is an animal and humans are humans. When a human being begins to exhibit the characteristics of an animal, it should be clear that something is wrong somewhere. Wherever you see a man manifesting whatever God did not create with a man, it means another spirit which is contrary to the Spirit of God is in operation in the person. When you handle a spiritual problem with physical strategies, you are bound to make things worse or get no positive lasting result. Only animals resort to physical aggression to establish their dominance over the opposite sex, hence the act of domestic abuse is attributed to the spirit of the beast. The spirit of beast and aggression is demonic and can be cast out, no matter its source. Your spouse can change if you take him or her back to the creator of the heaven and the earth in prayers. Isaiah 11:6-7 says, "The wolf also shall dwell with the lamb, and the leopard shall lie down with the kid; and the calf and the young lion and the fatling together; and a little child shall lead them. And the cow and the bear shall feed; their young ones shall lie down together: and the lion shall eat straw like the ox."

Any man or woman that beats their spouse has a spirit of the beast of the field. This is not meant as an insult, but it is in the spirit of fair labelling, calling the truth what it is. The individuals are not the beast but the spirit in them.

They must be aware that God does fight for the oppressed. God cannot be happy with you if you handle His child violently. Jeremiah 9:24 says, "But let him that glorieth glory in this, that he understandeth and knoweth me, that I am the Lord which exercise lovingkindness, judgment, and righteousness, in the earth: for in these things I delight, saith the Lord."

It is very easy to conclude that the best solution to domestic violence is to involve the police, separate the abused from the abuser and eventually seek a divorce from them. Obviously, if your circumstance gets to a state where your life is under threat, you might need to take immediate measure to escape from imminent danger such as separating for a while. However, you must resist the mind-set to proceed this to permanent separation as such will be contrary to the will of God. The Lord says He hates divorce. Malachi 2:16 NLT says, "For I hate divorce!" says the Lord, the God of Israel. "To divorce your wife is to overwhelm her with cruelty," says the Lord of Heaven's Armies. "So guard your heart; do not be unfaithful to your wife."

The cogent point is that seeking lawful restraint and eviction of the abuser does not provide a permanent solution to the problem. This is because the abusive partner you divorce still carries the spirit in them, and may eventually marry again with the same demonic disposition causing someone else to be their victim. This only multiplies victims. Someone who really loves their spouse and recognises that their spouse is under the manipulation of the wrong spirit, will need to help them through this period of their life. It may have to be done from a safe distance if that is what it takes, particularly where violence is involved.

Questions To Answer To Determine The Root Of Violence.

Before you can help as the helper you are called to be and overcome the affliction together, you will need to answer the questions below in order to identify the root cause of your spouse's behaviour.

SOME QUESTIONS YOU NEED TO ANSWER:

1. Did the abuse start before you got married?
2. Is the violent act always triggered by certain behaviour?
3. Does the violence happen suddenly without any physical triggers and the perpetrator regrets it as soon as the crisis is over?
4. Does the perpetrator remain arrogant and unrepentant after the act of violence?
5. Does the violent act get triggered by a mental illness crisis?
6. Have you asked him/her why he/she is aggressive and what's the reaction?
7. Do you know the family background, if your spouse came from abusive background?

If you can answer the above questions, then you are on the way to finding the solution to you and your spouse's problem.

The problems that apply to your spouse's situation will determine the actions you need to take to put an end to the abuse. A caring spouse who recognises or rightfully diagnoses the root of the violent behaviour in their partner can go through the challenge till there's a solution with the help of God. If you need extra support from charity organisations that deal with domestic violence, please do seek support, but have it in mind that the permanent solution is from God. In whatever action you take, you must believe that God is the ultimate. God is the only one who can bring a solution to every challenge of life. With men, it is impossible but with God all things are possible. Human beings might have temporary or second class solutions, but God has the original and permanent solution. Walk with God in this and you shall have a testimony. The wolf man you see today can become a lamb tomorrow. The terrible spouse you see today might be a great asset tomorrow.

Job 5:23-24 says, "For thou shalt be in league with the stones of the field: and the beasts of the field shall be at peace with thee. And thou shalt know that thy tabernacle shall be in peace; and thou shalt visit thy habitation, and shalt not sin." This scripture is the plan of God for you, to turn your aggressive spouse to a peaceful man. But you must make sure that you are not the author or the deliberate provoker of the act of violence. Work on your own anger and any areas of your life that can trigger violence.

NOTE:

Please, understand that there have been cases of domestic violence where both partners have worked together to bring the best out of the violent spouse and shed off the violence. Be reassured that although there might be need for temporary separation, divorce does not have to be the ultimate solution.

How To Handle The Abuse That Started Before You Got Married.

At the beginning of this book, it was mentioned that domestic violence is a deadly virus that has led to many untimely deaths, permanent damage and divorce which God declared that He hates.

Domestic violence is not something to be taken for granted. Further deaths can be avoided if we understand that neither divorce nor incarceration are solutions to domestic violence. The root cause must be dealt with. Otherwise, someone else will die the death that you avoided by chasing the man out. Chasing the man out is not even a guarantee that he will not come back to haunt you or inflict even more grievous damage. Cases have been recorded where the violent ex-spouse eventually killed the ex-wife. Therefore separation does not mean permanent safety.

In the previous chapter, we looked at some questions to consider in order to identify the root cause of your spouse's behaviour. Now, we will visit each question in detail.

QUESTION 1. Did the abuse start before you got married?

What do you do if the man was physically abusing you before you got married, but you still went ahead to marry him?

It must be a normal courtship practice that both involved in a relationship divulge any negative traits in their family to each other, so that each party will be able to make an informed decision as to whether or not they want to proceed with the relationship. If they choose to stay in the relationship, both parties must utilize the time of courtship to pray out every negative traits in their families, as well as subdue and draw the bloodline so that history will not repeat itself in their home.

You should not have married someone who you knew was violent. If you married someone who physically abused you when in courtship, be sure that he will potentially continue to abuse you when you get married. Let it be known to you that you cannot change any man by the dint of your ability.

If the root of problem is not dealt with, the problem will get worse. The root will determine what measures you need to take to solve it. If a headache is caused by dehydration, the treatment you'll give will be different from the headache caused by high blood pressure. Treating the headache and not treating the blood pressure will not take away the blood pressure, which means that the illness will worsen and can cause permanent damage or untimely death if not treated. If your friend tells you that she was going through the same domestic violence and gives you advice on how to overcome yours, it might not work for you because the root cause of your issue might be different.

A man who has started beating you before you got married does not deserve you. However, if you are already married to him, be advised that you need the word of God (and not the mere word of men) in order to fight this battle permanently.

WHAT DO I DO?

1. You need to first recognise that you are in an abusive relationship, that it is abnormal and that you need help.

    You need the help of God first. You will also need to speak to someone you can trust, who can stand with you in prayer and in general support until the solution comes. Such person may be your spiritual leader or someone you are led to, by the Holy Spirit.

2. You need to develop a mind-set whereby you cannot live with violence and it has to be eradicated. If you think you can manage it or think you can live with it forever, your life may be cut short in the process. You will live in fear of the unknown for the rest of your life and the children raised under such an atmosphere may turn out to be future tyrants. Children become what they see and the happenings in the home influence them greatly. For these reasons, you need to make a decision not to be comfortable living with domestic violence.

3. God should be your first point of contact and your first source of help. That is why you need to fast and pray that God will open your eyes to know the root of your spouse's problem. Violent nature is always traceable to a root. God did not create us to be violent. Everything He created was good. Once you know the root, then the solution is possible. It is compulsory to persevere knowing the root of your spouse's abusive/violent nature. The violence or beating is not the problem, but it is the root cause of the violent nature. Hebrews 12:15 NLT says, "Look after each other so that none of you fails to receive the grace of God. Watch out that no poisonous root of bitterness grows up to trouble you, corrupting many."

4. Don't allow the height or depth of the root of the violence to scare you. There is no root too deep or too strong that God cannot reach. Malachi 4:1 says, "For, behold, the day cometh, that shall burn as an oven; and all the proud, yea, and all that do wickedly, shall be stubble: and the day that cometh shall burn them up, saith the Lord of hosts, that it shall leave them neither root nor branch."

Moreover, the Bible says in Jeremiah 1:10 KJV, "See, I have this day set thee over the nations and over the kingdoms, to root out, and to pull down, and to destroy, and to throw down, to build, and to plant."

You have been made to have dominion over all things, to be able to root out and destroy any form of evil root. You are bigger than any root of violence.

POSSIBLE ROOTS OF VIOLENT CONDUCT

- It might be that he was raised in an abusive home, where his dad used to beat his mum, or mum beats the dad or he may have been abused as well.
- It might be that he has a low self-esteem, caused by bullying and always wants to cover up by being in control.
- It might be traceable to an issue in his family lineage.
- It might be an expression of jealousy to claim ownership of the person.
- It might be diabolical.
- It might be an expression of unforgiveness or bitterness due to what the spouse did before marriage or after.

Prayerfully ask him why he beats you. Don't assume that your perception is right. You might be surprised. God may touch his heart to share with you his background experience which may have influenced his mind-set and emotions, or which had turned him to be a violent person. Sometimes, the violent partner may not even know why they are being violent, but God can reveal it to you so that you can treat the root and not the symptoms.

Daniel 2:22 KJV says, "He revealeth the deep and secret things: he knoweth what is in the darkness, and the light dwelleth with him."

Mark 4:22 HCSB says, "For nothing is concealed except to be revealed, and nothing hidden except to come to light."

You might need to eliminate the causes one by one, when addressing and dealing with the root.

HOW TO DEAL WITH THE ROOT OF VIOLENT BEHAVIOUR CAUSED BY VIOLENT BACKGROUND.

• If the reason is as a result of being raised in a home where domestic violence was prevalent, you need to be patient, pray and introduce him to the word of God that will renew his mind.

• Look for scriptures that will change his thinking. If his mindset changes, he will change. The damage that was done has set his mind up for violence. His mind has been programmed for violence due to the violent nature he was exposed to.

• If he is born again, paste the written or printed word of God in strategic areas of the house where you know he will see it. If he is not born again, pray for his salvation. Old things will be passed away in his life and all things shall become new. Hebrews 4:12 says, "For the word of God is quick, and powerful, and sharper than any two-edged sword, piercing even to the dividing asunder of soul and spirit, and of the joints and marrow, and is a discerner of the thoughts and intents of the heart."

Romans 12:2 says, "And be not conformed to this world: but be ye transformed by the renewing of your mind, that ye may prove what is that good, and acceptable, and perfect, will of God."

● Paste scriptures such as love is kind, what love is about, do not deal treacherously with the wife of your youth, etc. Only the word of God can wash away the violent nature that has been programmed into him.

HOW TO DEAL WITH VIOLENT ROOT CAUSED BY LOW SELF ESTEEM.

● If the cause of the violence is low self-esteem, you need to work on respect and honouring your spouse. Let him know that he is important and has been created in the image of God. If your spouse's self-esteem has been damaged by negative words, you will need to use positive words to build him/her up. Be determined to make him/her feel important. You need a lot of patience and selflessness to help them overcome their violent behaviour. Do not expect the effect of negative words or negative actions that has been sown into his life to disappear in a day. You need to continue speaking the positive and lifting words into his life until you see a change. Job 14:14 says, "If a man die, shall he live again? All the days of my appointed time, will I wait, till my change come." Your own positive words will become like water that will wash away negative words he was raised up to believe. Every positive words you speak into his/her life is a seed which will eventually manifest. What he/she manifest now is as a result of the negative seed of words and actions which was sown into his/her life.

Proverbs 12:18 NLT says, "Some people make cutting remarks, but the words of the wise bring healing."

1 Peter 2:9 KJV says, "But ye are a chosen generation, a royal priesthood, an holy nation, a peculiar people; that ye should shew forth the praises of him who hath called you out of darkness into his marvellous light."

• The word of your mouth can give him a new mind-set. Don't call him what you are seeing. Call him who you want him to be.

• Get books that can minister to him personally as a valuable and unique human being.

HOW TO DEAL WITH VIOLENT ROOT CAUSED BY LINEAGE ISSUES.

There are happenings in life that are rooted in generational curses or occurrences. There is no other solution to this kind of violence than to break the generational link and draw the blood line. Psalms 11:3 KJV, If the foundations be destroyed, what can the righteous do?

This generational yoke can only be broken by giving your life to Jesus Christ, fasting and prayer. Nothing else can bring the solution.

Matthew 17:21 KJV says, "Howbeit this kind goeth not out but by prayer and fasting." If possible, ask him to join you in prayers. Be warned, he might not believe he has a problem to pray about, but you know why you are doing what you are doing. You are in his life as a helper. Help him with the right solution. Know that if you were the one in such situation, you would need someone to stand out to help you too. He cannot help himself.

Colossians 3:23 KJV says, "And whatsoever ye do, do it heartily, as to the Lord, and not unto men."

HOW TO DEAL WITH VIOLENCE CAUSED BY UNFORGIVENESS/BITTERNESS.

Bitterness is a deadly poison which can both cause harm to the person who has it and the person you are bitter towards. If the violent behaviour is an expression of unforgiveness or bitterness as a result of what the other spouse did to offend them, then you need to ask for forgiveness. Pray for the perpetrator that they will no longer walk in the spirit of unforgiveness and bitterness. Hebrews 12:15 KJV states "Looking diligently lest any man fail of the grace of God; lest any root of bitterness springing up trouble you, and thereby many be defiled"

I heard about a man who made up his mind to make the spouse's life miserable because he realised on their wedding day that she wasn't a virgin that she claimed to be. The wife was not aware of the root of the hatred and violence towards her. All she knew was that her marriage has been hell since she got married. When the wife opened up about what she was going through in the hands of her husband and their Pastor got involved, the man kept the reason for his violent act a secret. Once the root was exposed, both of them were able to reconcile and that was the end of domestic violence in their home. There's always a root. Deal with the root and you will see the back of domestic violence.

Violence Induced By Triggers.

Is the violent behaviour always triggered by certain behaviours?

Domestic violence is a virus you cannot afford to live with. It is a virus because it doesn't affect the carrier only, but causes harm and damages to all the people around. It is contagious because if someone is violent towards you, you will want to defend yourself and in the process you become violent as well, be it verbally or physically. Everyone in the house will share in its toxic nature one way or the other. The way to a permanent solution is for both parties to identify the root of the violent nature and deal with it.

Despite any excuses which may be given for the cause or the trigger for the violence, it must also be affirmed that no one deserves to be treated like an animal. Violence is never a good way to handle issues or to correct one another. There is nothing your spouse can do that should excuse your violent conduct towards them. James 1:19-20 HCSB says, "my dearly loved brothers, understand this: Everyone must be quick to hear, slow to speak, and slow to anger, for man's anger does not accomplish God's righteousness."

Nevertheless, if your spouse's violent act is always triggered by certain behaviour from you, then you are the solution to the root of the problem. One of the behaviours that can make a man be violent towards his wife, although it is not acceptable, is when the woman displays a very sharp tongue. As much as having a sharp tongue does not give the man the right to lay hands on you, at the same time, you must watch your tongue. This issue is further treated below.

WHAT ARE THE BEHAVIOURS THAT CAN TRIGGER VIOLENCE IN A SPOUSE?

1. Dishonouring and disrespecting your spouse can trigger violent act.

If you are one who does not respect or honour your husband, particularly if you know quite well that this person has an anger issue, then it can lead to violent acts. It is best if you learn how to respect and honour your spouse. That might even be all you need, to put a perpetual end to that virus of violence in your home.

If the root of the abusive problem is low self-esteem and he was never reckoned with it when he was growing up, he may now want to command respect at any cost. The result of this can be violent conduct. The Bible urges us to respect and honour our spouse and this is not too much to ask for. A sure way to help the situation is by offering your spouse the undiluted honour and respect they crave for. It is a tried and tested marital solution that is scriptural.

The solution is in your hands and not in the hands of any therapist. When such men leave their original marriage where they have shown violent traits and go on to marry someone else who respects and honours them and does not verbally abuse them, you will be surprised at the changes that will take place in their behaviour. This means, the antidotes to their violent behaviour is respect and honour.

Ephesians 5:33 HCSB says, "To sum up, each one of you is to love his wife as himself, and the wife is to respect her husband". It is biblical to respect your husband. Your spouse should not need to beg for respect in order for you to show respect. The Bible says, 'Respect'. A man would forfeit food for respect. No matter how delicious the food you put on your husband's table is, if you don't respect him, you are like a thorn in his heart. Even if he does things that make him not to command respect, you should respect him because the Bible says so. God will look at your act of obedience to His word and answer your prayers. Two wrongs do not make a right. Remember, we are on the journey to kill the root of violence.

1 Peter 3:1-2 ESV says, "Likewise, wives, be subject to your own husbands, so that even if some do not obey the word, they may be won without a word by the conduct of their wives, when they see your respectful and pure conduct."

Please, ask for the grace to respect and honour your husband, to save your life from being cut short, and to help your husband to be free of that deadly virus of violence. Ask for the grace so that you won't raise up another tyrant in your children, who may grow up to be violent to their spouse and others in their community.

2. Verbal abuse.

Many do not know that verbal abuse is as dangerous and damaging as physical abuse, or even more dangerous. The effect of physical abuse is so obvious to all. People will see the broken arms, and swollen eyes. However, no one can see the damage that has been done emotionally by a sharp and dangerous tongue, which may eventually lead the victim to commit suicide. James 3:3, 8 KJV says, "But the tongue can no man tame; it is an unruly evil, full of deadly poison." Both men and women are guilty of this. If you are one that verbally abuses your spouse, you might actually be the root of his abusive nature. No man enjoys it when his wife verbally abuses him and no woman likes it either. Proverbs 18:6 says, "a fool's lips bring strife, and his mouth calls for blows."

The bible in Job 5:21 mentioned about the scourge of the tongue. A scourge is a whip used as an instrument of punishment, designed to cause great suffering. A person who employs their mouth to verbally abuse their spouse is not much better than the person who physically abuses them. Men are not naturally endowed with the gift of the garb, that is, they seldom command the same verbal ability as a woman. Hence some may violently react in retaliation if they suffer the persistent scourge of the tongue from their spouse. Just as children with speech impediments would react in the playground because they couldn't express their opinion in clear words, in the same way, some men resort to their fists in their anger. Both of you are using your negative power to hurt each other. You have the power of the tongue and he has the power of the fist. Both acts are ungodly and damaging to the temple of God. 1 Corinthians 6:19-20 ESV says, "Or do you not know that your body is a temple of the Holy Spirit within you, whom you have from God?" You are not your own, for you were bought with a price. So glorify God in your body. Verbally and physically abusing your spouse shows that you don't honour God. This is because your words of abuse are designed to reduce them below who God has made them. Also, their physical abuse to your body is an offense to God.

Here's what the bible says about quarrelsome women.

- Proverbs 21:19 NLT, It's better to live alone in the desert than with a quarrelsome, complaining wife.
- Proverbs 26:21 NLT, A quarrelsome person starts fights as easily as hot embers light charcoal or fire lights wood.
- James 1:26 NLT, If you claim to be religious but don't control your tongue, you are fooling yourself, and your religion is worthless.

No matter how many times you carry your Bible in a day or how many titles you have as a minister of God, if you are engaged in verbal abuse towards your spouse, your religion is vain.

3. Being rude to his parents.

Being rude to someone younger than you or your colleague is bad enough, but it is worse when you extend that rudeness to those older than you, especially your spouse's parents. This act is ungodly. It does not matter how their own attitude is. You have no right or justification to be rude to your in-laws. You may need to know what is written in the book of Mark 10:7-9 ESV, 'Therefore a man shall leave his father and mother and hold fast to his wife, and the two shall become one flesh.' So they are no longer two but one flesh. What therefore God has joined together, let not man separate. From the moment that you and your spouse have become one, your parents become his and his parents become yours. If you cannot adhere to this instruction of two becoming one in the Bible, please don't bother to get married to someone whose parents you cannot accept as yours, because the consequences are more dangerous than physical violence. The first commandment with a promise that God gave, was in line with honouring our parents. Ephesians 6:2-3 KJV says, "Honour thy father and mother; (which is the first commandment with promise); That it may be well with thee, and thou mayest live long on the earth."

If you think your in-law does not deserve to be honoured and you dishonour them, it will definitely trigger the violent act in your spouse. Think of the more destructive consequences that are attached to your disobedience to God's commandment, which says you should honour them. You don't want your life to be cut short because of disobedience to the word of God.

4. Infidelity

Infidelity is the act of sexual unfaithfulness to your spouse. This involves you having an affair with the opposite sex, who has become the third party in your marriage. This is an act of disrespect, unfaithfulness, betrayal, disregard and insensitivity which can bring about anger, distrust, resentment, hatred, disrespect in return etc. This can bring about the act of violence from either the woman or the man who has been betrayed. Any party who cannot handle the act of Infidelity will result to being violent to the culprit. There have been stories of women and men who have damaged or killed their spouse because of infidelity. Please control yourself because it is very damaging. If you think your spouse is not sufficient for you sexually and you're being tempted to seek sexual satisfaction outside your marriage, think twice. If you wish to satisfy yourself by engaging in an act of infidelity, think twice and respect God by honouring His 7th commandment which says, "Thou shalt not commit adultery". Also, consider this. The eternal consequences you will suffer which are more dangerous than the consequence of physical abuse which you receive from your spouse. 1 Corinthians 6:9-10 KJV says, "Know ye not that the unrighteous shall not inherit the kingdom of God? Be not deceived: neither fornicators, nor idolaters, nor adulterers, nor effeminate, nor abusers of themselves with mankind, nor thieves, nor covetous, nor drunkards, nor revellers, nor extortioners, shall inherit the kingdom of God". The earthly consequences you get from this act is nothing compared with the eternal consequence if you die or you are killed in this sinful state of mind.

However, no matter how much you have been betrayed by your spouse, it should not be resolved with physical abuse to the extent that you may cause them permanent or temporary injury. There are other ways to handle situations other than resulting to violence. Hand them over to the one who created them and has the power to change them. Infidelity is a thing of the heart which has its own root as well. The most obvious root cause of infidelity is lack of the fear of God. It will take God to change them.

There are many triggers of domestic violence and we have been exposed to the knowledge that there is always a root which definitely needs to be dealt with. However, while working on how to deal with the root, we must do our best not to trigger our spouse's violence act by the above behaviours.

Violence Without Trigger.

Does the violence start suddenly without any trigger? Does the party express remorse and regrets immediately after the act? Does that individual appear to be in a trance?

There have been situations where the spouse would suddenly become aggressive for some time, then would immediately regret the action. Irrespective of the manner or cause of the violence towards you, be determined to see violence as a deadly virus. Deal with this virus as early as the first day it happened. It is better to deal with this promptly. Some people have been living with abusive relationship for ten years and they have not done anything about it. God did not create you to be handled violently. 1 Peter 3:7 KJV says, "Likewise, ye husbands, dwell with them according to knowledge, giving honour unto the wife, as unto the weaker vessel, and as being heirs together of the grace of life; that your prayers be not hindered".

You are meant to be treated delicately and not violently, so stop thinking it is normal to be beaten. Do not think that because as a child, you witnessed your mum being beaten, and she never told anyone and she coped with it, that it is normal to be physically abused. It is not normal neither is it right. You might have been told that abuse or violence is normal in marriage. Do not buy into this lie. It is a lie of the devil to have you live a miserable life when it does not have to be so. There is a solution.

From the first time your spouse uses his/her hands or any object to physically abuse you, let that individual know that you will not allow this kind of behaviour. Let them know that they will need to seek help in order to stop that attitude, or else there will be separation. Beware though, that this might not work immediately on someone who is being diabolically controlled. In such a case, you will need to prayerfully work together on that issue. Ephesians 6:12 says, "For we wrestle not against flesh and blood, but against principalities, against powers, against the rulers of the darkness of this world, against spiritual wickedness in high places." You may need to separate for some time as your life may be in danger. While you do this, please do not set your mind on putting a permanent end to the relationship.

There are circumstances where some women employed diabolical power in order to force a man into marriage. Some have also used diabolical power to steal some men out of their matrimonial home. Eventually, when the diabolical runs out of steam and its power expires, and the man's eyes will be opened and he would not comprehend how he ended up being with the woman. If you have been one of the above mentioned women, the best solution is to let the man go back to his home. If he was single when you met him and you engaged him diabolically, your lot will be up to the mercy of God. If he doesn't want to be with you, let him go before he kills you in the house one day.

Now, let's revisit the question: Does the violence start suddenly without any trigger? Does the party express remorse and regrets immediately after the act? Does that individual appear to be in a trance?

If someone you had been laughing with, suddenly turns around and starts beating you for no just cause, then you must know that there is more to it than meets the eye. It may be that this person is being remotely controlled. I have heard stories about men that will not know why they beat their wives, but they just did. It was then found out later that some enchantment was enacted against the union by an ex-girlfriend who had obtained the diabolical means to exert revenge. There have been stories of men being demonically influenced to self-inflict damage to their own marriage by acts of violence.

There are some people whose family members do not want them to have a happy home. They may evoke enchantment in the spirit realm so that when the husband sees the wife, the image she portrays will disgust him. She might be beautiful physically, but to the man, she will look irritating and far from alluring. Many true stories abound. There was one where the mother enchanted the son to continually beat his wife, so that they can go their separate ways because the person he married wasn't the mum's choice.

Some people have a spirit husband or a spirit wife, where such demonic spouse may be influencing the happenings in the home with the sole aim of ending the marriage. Sometimes we allow little issues in the marriage to trigger violence, thereby dancing to their tunes and helping them to facilitate the establishment of their aims by throwing our spouses out of the house.

Some people are operating under generational marital curses. If your eyes are opened to what is happening in the spirit realm you will handle an abusive situation differently. It is therefore an effort of futility to attempt to solve spiritual issues with physical remedies. The beginning of the solution to the issue is seeking to know the root cause and to deal with it prayerfully.

WHAT DO I DO?

1. You must be determined not to tolerate this abuse and believe that it has to come to an end. Matthew 18:18 KJV says, "Verily I say unto you, whatsoever ye shall bind on earth shall be bound in heaven: and whatsoever ye shall loose on earth shall be loosed in heaven."

2. You must be aware that if you know for sure that your husband really loves you and that he is not normally an angry person, then the abuse is

diabolical. Ephesians 6:12 KJV says, "For we wrestle not against flesh and blood, but against principalities, against powers, against the rulers of the darkness of this world, against spiritual wickedness in high places."

If you are born again, then you will need to discern when a battle is spiritual and not mere physical. If you are not born again, your number one self-responsibility is to become born again. Open the door of your heart to Jesus. If you are to enrol in an institution, then you would want to familiarise yourself with the proprietor who will give you directions on how to navigate through the school successfully. If you don't, you might not come out with good results. It is the same in the spiritual.

If you are born again as a woman and you don't have the spirit of discernment, then you need to pray for it. You need it in your journey through life. You cannot do this assignment blindly. The spirit of discernment will identify every doing that is not genuine despite how good it looks. You will definitely know when things are not going right in your home. There will be no surprises. Hebrews 5:14 ESV says, "But solid food is for the mature, for those who have their powers of discernment trained by constant practice to distinguish good from evil."

3. Ask God to reveal to you the root cause of the violence. Daniel 2:22 says, "He revealeth the deep and secret things: he knoweth what is in the darkness, and the light dwelleth with him". Until you know the root or source of a problem, you may not have a solution for it. If God can show you the root, then the end of the violence will come.

4. Fast and pray before you approach your husband on discussing the issue. It makes a huge difference when God touches the heart of a man, Proverbs

21:1 says, "The king's heart is in the hand of the Lord, as the rivers of water: he turneth it whithersoever he will."

You don't have to do much work when God has touched your spouse's heart. If you approach your husband with God's wisdom and favour which you have obtained through prayer, you will definitely see the travail of your soul and be glad. However, if you handle it foolishly by shouting and exchanging verbal insult with a person who is being demonically influenced, you will have negative results.

Esther 5:2 says, "And it was so, when the king saw Esther the queen standing in the court, that she obtained favour in his sight: and the king held out to Esther the golden sceptre that was in his hand. Esther drew near, and touched the top of the sceptre." Esther obtained favour after she had fasted and prayed. Don't underestimate the power of prayer.

5. Encourage your spouse to join you in fasting and prayer. You can also request for your Pastor's involvement or someone who Holy Spirit leads you to ask. Matthew 18:19-20 says, "Again I say unto you, that if two of you shall agree on earth as touching anything that they shall ask, it shall be done for them of my Father which is in heaven. For where two or three are gathered together in my name, there am I in the midst of them ". If your spouse doesn't want to join in the prayer, please go ahead without them. Stand in agreement with your Pastor or that person who the Holy Spirit has directed you to. Remember, your spouse is the one who needs deliverance and the devil will not want him delivered. Hence he may be influenced to resist the suggestion of prayer. Remain in prayer until God has touched his heart.

6. After the deliverance, seek marital counselling as your marital concept or mind-set may have been manipulated diabolically from the beginning. Psalms 11:3 says, "If the foundations be destroyed, what can the righteous do?" Therefore, you may need a renewing of mind in order to know the principles of God concerning marriage. Proverbs 19:2 says, "Also, that the soul be without knowledge, it is not good; and he that hasteth with his feet sinneth".

7. Prayerfully guard your home against further demonic manipulation. They might want to fight back since their deeds were exposed and stopped. When Jesus overcame Satan's temptation, the bible states that he left him for an opportune time. Become an intercessor for your spouse and children. Zechariah 9: 8 says, "But I will encamp at my temple to guard it against marauding forces. Never again will an oppressor overrun my people, for now I am keeping watch."

8. If the cause is as a result of the woman having demonic, disfavoured, and disgusting spiritual garments on them, the same procedure applies. Prayer and fasting is the solution. Ask for new garments of beauty, attraction, favour and honour. Zechariah 3: 4 says, "And he answered and spake unto those that stood before him, saying, Take away the filthy garments from him. And unto him he said, Behold, I have caused thine iniquity to pass from thee, and I will clothe thee with change of raiment".

9. If you do have children, then both parents need to debrief the children and prayerfully wash their minds with the word of God and prayer. The altercations in the home may have left them with a wrong view of marriage. This may have been built up in them because of the violent acts which they have been exposed to. The exercise of deliberately talking with

them and putting an end to the hostilities in their environment will forestall the transfer of such negative trait to their future. If their experience had influenced their misconception that domestic violence is a way of life, then you owe them the duty to correct such warped impression. Teach them the word of God and allow the new loving and Godly behaviour between you and your spouse to renew their mind-set. Hebrews 4:12 states, "For the word of God is quick, and powerful, and sharper than any two-edged sword, piercing even to the dividing asunder of soul and spirit, and of the joints and marrow, and is a discerner of the thoughts and intents of the heart." Romans 12:2 says, "And be not conformed to this world: but be ye transformed by the renewing of your mind, that ye may prove what is that good, and acceptable, and perfect, will of God."

NOTE

Knowledge is power. If you do not know the root of a problem, you will probably apply wrong remedy and will not solve the problem. If your car has engine problem and you are fixing the brake, the problem will linger until the engine is destroyed. But if you take it to the mechanics and they are able to detect the problem, they will treat it and you will not have engine breakdown. Take the issues in your marriage to God, the author of marriage, and you will not be disappointed.

Does Your Spouse Remain Arrogant And Unrepentant After The Act Of Violence?

To those who are experiencing or witnessing this ugly situation, domestic violence can look like an insurmountable mountain. To the victims of violence in the home, it may sometimes look like there can never be an end to it. To some, it may look like a terminal disease that cannot be cured. Is there anything too hard for God to do? With man it may be impossible, but with God nothing shall be impossible.

Often times, those around us - relatives, friends, non-governmental organisations (NGOs), the government, etc., cause us to believe that the only obvious solution to domestic violence is to break up the family and run away from the house. That kind of approach is only sweeping a dangerous situation under the carpet. That's the easiest way out of the situation, but it's not the permanent solution. Such knee-jerk solution can only breed bitterness, uncertainty about the outcome, damaged children and much more. Of course, it may be wise to seek help, vacate the house or ask the abuser to leave, especially in circumstances where there is evidence of uncontrollable anger, violence or life endangerment. However, this should not be considered a permanent solution. There must be a genuine desire to seek a permanent solution where your spouse is being transformed.

The only way you can have a permanent solution is to seek the face of God to know the root of the violent behaviour and asking God to deal with the root. Both the victim and the culprit should seek the face of God. If you are the one that beats up your spouse, it's high time you know that you have a problem and it is abnormal to be violent towards your spouse. Any man or woman that raises their hands to beat their spouse must know that they have the spirit of beast in them. The bible says in Psalms 49:20, "Man that is in honour, and understands it not, is like the beasts that perish." God has called you to honour and not dishonour. Therefore, you must do everything to be delivered of this spirit. It is a deadly spirit which can devour the victim, destroy your family and frustrate your own destiny and possibly add a criminal record to the bargain. You are only allowing the devil to carry out his assignments through you. Say no to the devil and be free from his manipulation. John 10:10 says "The thief has come to kill, steal and destroy, but Jesus has come to give us abundant life". The devil only wants to use you to kill the joy in your home, steal and destroy what God has purposed for your home. Once you have been used, you will be dumped.

Does your husband remain arrogant and unrepentant after the act of violence?

Being arrogant and having an unrepentant heart are obviously not godly virtues. Any behaviour or attitude that cannot be identified with the fruit of the Spirit will definitely be identified with the fruits of the flesh. The person you serve determines what you manifest. Galatians 5:19-21 says, "Now the works of the flesh are manifest, which are these; Adultery, fornication, uncleanness, lasciviousness, Idolatry, witchcraft, hatred, variance, emulations, wrath, strife, seditions, heresies, envying, murders, drunkenness, revelling, and such like: of the which I tell you before, as I have also told you in time past, that they do such things shall not inherit the kingdom of God".

One of the fruits of the flesh is 'wrath' which is a vital ingredient that can lead to domestic violence.

WHAT IS WRATH?

Wrath can be defined as a strong vengeful anger or indignation or very great anger. Synonyms of wrath are anger, annoyance, temper, mood, rage, fury and acrimony. Uncontrollable anger is what normally gives birth to violence. This anger will not only affect your marital life but can leave you jobless. It can cause diseases in your body, such as high blood pressure, depression and other disorders. Anger releases poisonous toxins into the bloodstream which can cause various disorders in the body.

Some people do not fit in any of these categories – are diabolically controlled, were abused when they were little, were brought up in a domestic violent home, or are mentally ill. Nonetheless, they are still violent. For these people, the reason for their anger and ignition of violence lies within them. They have lost control of their flesh. They live in the flesh whereby they obey the voice of their flesh, which causes them not to suffer fools gladly or tolerate nonsense from anybody. It is dangerous to dance to the tune of your flesh as there are negative consequences not only here on earth, but much more eternal consequences. The truth is, those who cannot control their anger cannot inherit the kingdom of God. Ephesians 4:26 says, "Be ye angry, and sin not; let not the sun go down upon your wrath." Moses in the Bible missed the Promised Land because he could not control his anger. The Bible did not say don't be angry, but you must have the power to control your anger, so that you will not sin.

Galatians 6:7-8 says, "Be not deceived; God is not mocked: for whatsoever a man soweth, that shall he also reap. For he that soweth to his flesh shall of the flesh reap corruption; but he that soweth to the Spirit shall of the Spirit reap life everlasting." Anytime you obey the voice of your flesh, you have sown loyalty, confidence and sense of ownership to your flesh. If your spouse chooses to obey the voice of the flesh by displaying anger which leads to physical abuse, then the root of his violent nature could be traced to his spirituality . In that case, the solution to his problem is to live by the Spirit. Galatians 5:16 says, "This I say then, Walk in the Spirit, and ye shall not fulfil the lust of the flesh". Deal with an angry man with meekness and stand in gap for him until God changes his life. Unless he becomes physically violent, you don't need to leave the house. 2 Timothy 2:25-26 says, "In meekness instructing those that oppose themselves; if God peradventure will give them repentance to the acknowledging of the truth; And that they may recover themselves out of the snare of the devil, who are taken captive by him at his will".

Let your violent spouse realise that they need to seek the face of God for their anger issue. Reassure them of your support and readiness to join them in prayer. However, if they are becoming physically aggressive, it is advisable to inform your Pastor or a trusted prayer partner of their behaviour. The purpose of this is so that they can join you in prayer. Moses was so spiritual but the only reason he missed the Promised Land was because of anger. If the violent party needs to go for anger management therapy along with fasting and praying, please encourage him to do so. An angry man is a dangerous man. Some people are pathologically angry in nature. They need deliverance but you must constantly avoid doing thing to trigger the anger. Also, be aware that sometimes you don't need to do anything wrong to trigger their anger.

Drunkenness is also listed among the fruit of the flesh, and some spouses only physically abuse their spouse when they are drunk. Such cases have their roots in carnality, which one of the manifestations is drunkenness which then lead to violence. The fruit you manifest determines whether you live in the Spirit or live in the flesh. Hence attention should be paid to their spirituality. When they invite the Holy Spirit of God to dwell within them and then start listening to the Holy Spirit, they will stop hearing the voices of the flesh. This will be the end to the problem.

This book is not written only for the attention of victims of domestic violence, but also for the perpetrators. If no one has ever told you before, please be aware that abusing your spouse is a sure sign that you are suffering from a form of mental issue. Until you recognise your violent conduct as an offshoot of mental malfunction, you will not seek a solution. It is not a proof of strength, but a demonstration of weakness. A weak man cannot control his anger, but shows his weakness by beating his spouse. In the same way, a weak woman cannot control her tongue but damages and angers her spouse with her dangerous tongue. Not being able to control your tongue is a sign of weakness not strength.

Does Your Spouse Have Mental Illness?

Mental illness may or may not be the root cause of your spouse's violence. According to (Alexadra 2015) "a common assumption we hear at The Hotline is that abuse is caused by a partner's mental health condition, for example: bipolar disorder, depression, anxiety, post-traumatic stress disorder (PTSD), narcissistic personality, borderline personality or antisocial personality. While these are serious mental health conditions, they do not *cause* abuse. Nothing in the Diagnostic and Statistical Manual of Mental Disorders, fifth edition (DSM 5) states that a mental illness is the sole reason for a partner to be abusive in a relationship. However, there are a select few diagnoses which can increase the risk of abusive patterns showing up in a relationship and other areas of life. Mental illness tends to impact all areas of a person's life, such as work, interactions with friends, family engagement and personal relationships".

From the quote, one can deduce that mental illness does not necessarily cause domestic violence on its own. The same article suggested that mental illness and domestic violence should be treated separately. Therefore, apart from the advice presented in this book, it is suggested that you handle mental health spiritually along with professional help. With God, all things are possible. Your spouse does not have to die with mental illness. If your faith says yes, God will not say no. What He did before He can still do it again. Luke 8:26-29 narrated how a chronic mad man was healed permanently. We were made to understand that mental ailment is demonic and you can cast out the spirit.

Here's how you deal with mental illness:

- Make sure you have the authority to cast out demons. Luke 10:19 KJV states, "Behold, I give unto you power to tread on serpents and scorpions, and over all the power of the enemy: and nothing shall by any means hurt you".

- You must be born again to cast out demons. Mark16:17-18 states "And these signs shall follow them that believe; In my name shall they cast out devils; they shall speak with new tongues; They shall take up serpents; and if they drink any deadly thing, it shall not hurt them; they shall lay hands on the sick, and they shall recover".

- Join your faith with your Pastor and someone of Spiritual maturity who can stand in gap for you. According to Matthew18:19 KJV "Again I say unto you, That if two of you shall agree on earth as touching anything that they shall ask, it shall be done for them of my Father which is in heaven".

- Reassure your spouse of your love and support for them, especially if it's a new diagnosis. Let them know that their newly diagnosed mental health will not change how you feel about them. Ephesians 4:29 KJV, states "Let no corrupt communication proceed out of your mouth, but that which is good to the use of edifying, that it may minister grace unto the hearers".

- Don't cause them to feel less adequate. Let them know that the grace of God is sufficient for them. 2 Corinthians12:9 KJV states, "And he said unto me, My grace is sufficient for thee: for my strength is made perfect in weakness. Most gladly therefore will I rather glory in my infirmities, that the power of Christ may rest upon me".

- Give them their due honour and respect irrespective of their ailment. Don't look at them with the eye of their new ailment. Look at them as a child of God who needs love and care. Romans 12:10 NLT states, "Love each other with genuine affection, and take delight in honouring each other". John 13:34 NLT adds "So now I am giving you a new commandment: Love each other. Just as I have loved you, you should love each other".

- If there is a mental crisis that is out of control, call for help from the mental health professionals while you continue to pray for them. If they become aggressive, call for help.

Effects of Domestic Violence.

EFFECT OF DOMESTIC VIOLENCE ON THE HOME SETTING.

1. Everyone in the home walks like they are walking on a time bomb.
2. There is always a feeling of uncertainty - questioning whether the smile now will turn to crying.
3. There is a feeling or fear in the atmosphere.
4. The atmosphere is always turgid.
5. There is an act of pretence.
6. Regular conflict in the home.
7. Family Separation.

THE EFFECT OF DOMESTIC VIOLENCE ON THE VICTIM.

- Anxiety: The victim of domestic violence lives in perpetual fear of the unknown because this individual is not sure when they will be the recipient of a blow to her face or a stab wound. This a terrible state to be in, perpetually.

- There are risks of temporary or permanent physical injury and even death. Anyone exposed to domestic violence is at risk of sustaining any sort of physical injury which may result to death. That is why anyone going through domestic violence must be determined not to live in that situation without doing anything about it. You must be bold enough to seek help. It does not just go away unless something is done.

- A victim of domestic violence is at risk of suffering from mental illness, such as depression. The effects of fear of the unknown and physical body injury are enough to cause depression for the victim.

- They are withdrawn from families and friends. The spouse will not want the victim to be close to or alone with anyone else, due to the fact that their violent act may be exposed. That is why they give excuses for not being able to attend family gatherings.

- They feel suffocated. The culprit does not give them a chance to breathe their own air, which means they do not have time for their own space. Every conversation they have with anyone else is being monitored. They are not allowed to have private discussion with members of their family and friends, they are constantly being monitored by their spouse.

- They are confused or indecisive due to being caught in between the fear of leaving their spouse and the children: They would have loved to walk away from the abuse but thinking about the children and their relationship. They don't know what to do.

- They are at risk of further danger if they leave the relationship for another: The culprit would not want the victim to leave and re-marry. Some would prefer for the victim to remain with them and never be with anyone else. There have been cases where the culprit has waited for several years after the spouse left them before they kill the victim.

- Their self-esteem becomes low. The beating and battering reduces their self-esteem causing them to think they have little or no value.

EFFECTS OF DOMESTIC VIOLENCE ON THE CHILDREN IN THE MARRIAGE.

1. They live in trepidation. They live in fear of potential and imminent violence. They are therefore anxious.
2. They may have psychological, emotional and behavioural problems. This can lead to poor school performance, aggression, bedwetting and isolation from friends.
3. They can be aggressive to their colleagues and mates.
4. They can end up being a spouse abuser too.
5. They might end up becoming being part of a gang. Some children have been deprived of fatherly care because the mother cannot look after them alone. Although damage might be inevitable if a child lives in such a violent environment, the damage is much more inevitable if the woman becomes a single parent. Sometimes they remarry and the new spouse abuses the child or children.
6. They might make up their mind not to marry.
7. Low self-esteem.
8. Emotional distress.
9. Less empathy and caring for others.
10. Drug and alcohol abuse.
11. Homelessness.
12. Living with a stranger. (Change of home)
13. According to Astbury .J et al 2000, "In a large US study it was found that exposure to four or more categories of adverse childhood experiences was associated with a 4-12-fold increased risk of alcoholism, drug abuse, depression and attempted suicide".

Every seed sown will surely germinate to bring about fruits for harvest. The seed of domestic abuse sown in a home will definitely have effects on everyone in that home. Domestic violence is a force of evil that finds its way to root itself into the lives of everyone in the environment. Its seeds germinate, its fruits becomes obvious and spread to next generation because they have eaten from the fruit of violence. This now forms a root in them and bring out fruits for the next generation again. If not stopped, it goes from generation to generation. History has been known to repeat itself unless the root is cut off. You would be surprised that your female child might reap the seed of wickedness you have sown, by beating up your spouse. Treat your wife the way you will like your daughter's husband to treat her. As a woman, treat your husband the way you would like your son's wife to treat him. The major way root of domestic violence is cut off is by praying with the word of God and intentionally desiring deliberate change.

Prayers To Break The Yoke Of Violence.

Prayers For The Home.

1. John 19:28, 30 KJV, "After this, Jesus knowing that all things were now accomplished, that the scripture might be fulfilled, saith, I thirst. When Jesus therefore had received the vinegar, he said, It is finished: and he bowed his head, and gave up the ghost".

   Every finished work of the wicked ones against the peace of God in my home, is nullified by the finished work of Jesus Christ on the cross of Calvary in Jesus name.

2. John 1:5 NLT, "The light shines in the darkness, and the darkness can never extinguish it".

   Let your light shine and expose every work of darkness that has been done to fuel violence in my home in Jesus name.

3. James 4:7 NLT, "So humble yourselves before God. Resist the devil, and he will flee from you".

   I resist every evil Spirit of violence and anger that has my home their abode in Jesus name.

4. Isaiah 60:18 KJV, "Violence shall no more be heard in thy land, wasting nor destruction within thy borders; but thou shalt call thy walls Salvation, and thy gates praise".

    I decree and declare that violence shall not be heard in my home any longer in Jesus name. I shut the gate of my home against violence in Jesus name.

5. Philippians 4:7 KJV, "And the peace of God, which passeth all understanding, shall keep your hearts and minds through Christ Jesus".

    O Lord, let your peace that passes all understanding reign in my home from now in Jesus name.

6. Jeremiah 1:5 KJV, "Before I formed thee in the belly I knew thee; and before thou camest forth out of the womb I sanctified thee, and I ordained thee a prophet unto the nations".

    O Lord, let my home begin to fulfil that purpose you have ordained for my home from the beginning of the world in Jesus name.

7. Psalm 7:9, Oh, let the wickedness of the wicked come to an end; but establish the just: for the righteous God trieth the hearts and reins.

    O Lord, let everything that represents the work of darkness that has been causing the wave of violence in my home, come to an end in Jesus name.

Prayers For Perpetrators Of Domestic Violence.

1. Revelation 3:20 KJV, "Behold, I stand at the door, and knock: if any man hear my voice, and open the door, I will come in to him, and will sup with him, and he with me".

    I invite Jesus, the prince of peace, into my heart. Forgive me of all my sins. I accept you as my Lord and saviour.

2. Proverbs 19:11 NLT, "Sensible people control their temper; they earn respect by overlooking wrongs".

    I receive the grace to be able to overlook wrong and to be able to control my temper in Jesus name.

3. James 1:19-20 NLT, "Understand this, my dear brothers and sisters: You must all be quick to listen, slow to speak, and slow to get angry. Human anger does not produce the righteousness God desires".

    I disallow everything in my life that does not produce the righteousness of God. I receive the Spirit of patience and peace in Jesus name.

4. Luke 10:19 KJV, "Behold, I give unto you power to tread on serpents and scorpions, and over all the power of the enemy: and nothing shall by any means hurt you".

    I take authority over every angry nature which has taken hold of my life in Jesus name.

5. Ephesians 4:26-27 NLT, "And don't sin by letting anger control you." Don't let the sun go down while you are still angry, for anger gives a foothold to the devil".

O Lord, let every foothold I have given to the devil because of anger in my life, be redeemed by the blood of Jesus.

6. Genesis 1:31 KJV, "And God saw everything that he had made, and, behold, it was very good. And the evening and the morning were the sixth day".

    God created everything in me to reveal His goodness and excellent Spirit. Everything that is not good in me, I cast you out in Jesus name.

7. Matthew 15:13 KJV, "But he answered and said, every plant, which my heavenly Father hath not planted, shall be rooted up".

    Every seed of violence that has been planted in me, even from my tender age, which has taken root and bearing the fruit of violence, God did not created you with me. I uproot you in Jesus name.

8. Colossians 3:8 KJV, "But now ye also put off all these; anger, wrath, malice, blasphemy, filthy communication out of your mouth".

    I receive the power to do away with anger in Jesus name.

9. Ephesians 4:31-32 KJV, "Let all bitterness, and wrath, and anger, and clamour, and evil speaking, be put away from you, with all malice: And be ye kind one to another, tender-hearted, forgiving one another, even as God for Christ's sake hath forgiven you".

    I rebuke the spirit of strife, bitterness, malice and evil speaking from my life and home. I invite Spirit of kindness, forgiveness and love into my heart and home in Jesus name.

10. Romans 12:17-18 KJV, "Recompense to no man evil for evil. Provide things honest in the sight of all men. If it be possible, as much as lieth in you, live peaceably with all men".

O Lord, I receive the grace to live at peace with my spouse and children, irrespective of situation and circumstances in Jesus name.

11. Psalms 11:5 NLT, "The Lord examines both the righteous and the wicked. He hates those who love violence".

    O Lord, I ask for your mercy for my act of violence. Instead of judgement that the violent ones deserves, please God grant me tender mercy in Jesus name.

12. Ephesians 5:28-29, "So ought men to love their wives as their own bodies. He that loveth his wife loveth himself. For no man ever yet hated his own flesh; but nourisheth and cherisheth it, even as the Lord the church"

    O Lord, Give me the grace to love my spouse as you have commanded in Jesus name.

13. Philippians 4:8 KJV,"Finally, brethren, whatsoever things are true, whatsoever things are honest, whatsoever things are just, whatsoever things are pure, whatsoever things are lovely, whatsoever things are of good report; if there be any virtue, and if there be any praise, think on these things".

    O Lord, every thought from my past that is making me to be violent to my spouse I wash away by the blood of Jesus. My thoughts from now shall be of good report, lovely things, good report, purity and things that are just in Jesus name.

14. Matthew 12:29 KJV, "Or else how can one enter into a strong man's house, and spoil his goods, except he first bind the strong man? and then he will spoil his house".

Matthew 18:18 KJV, "Verily I say unto you, whatsoever ye shall bind on earth shall be bound in heaven: and whatsoever ye shall loose on earth shall be loosed in heaven".

I bind the strongman of violence and anger from my life and home in Jesus name. I resist your presence in my life and home from this moment in Jesus name.

15. Mark 16:17 KJV, "And these signs shall follow them that believe; In my name shall they cast out devils; they shall speak with new tongues."

I cast out of my life and home every strongman of violence and anger in Jesus name.

16. Matthew 19:26 KJV, "But Jesus beheld them, and said unto them, With men this is impossible; but with God all things are possible".

O Lord, let the deliverance from violence that men think is not possible, become possible in my life in Jesus name.

Prayers For Children Who Have Witnessed Domestic Violence.

1. Psalms 127:3 KJV, "Lo, children are an heritage of the Lord: and the fruit of the womb is his reward".

    O Lord, deliver your heritage from the storm of violence.

2. 1 John 3:8 KJV, "He that committeth sin is of the devil; for the devil sinneth from the beginning. For this purpose the Son of God was manifested, that he might destroy the works of the devil".

    O Lord, destroy the seed of violence that has been planted into my child/children's life.

3. Isaiah 40:24 KJV, "Yea, they shall not be planted; yea, they shall not be sown: yea, their stock shall not take root in the earth: and he shall also blow upon them, and they shall wither, and the whirlwind shall take them away as stubble".

    Every effect of domestic violence in my children's lives are blown away by the whirlwind of God in Jesus name.

    Every seed of domestic violence that has been planted in my children by encounter, shall not take root in them in Jesus name.

4. Isaiah 49:25 KJV, "But thus saith the Lord, Even the captives of the mighty shall be taken away, and the prey of the terrible shall be delivered: for I will contend with him that contendeth with thee, and I will save thy children".

    O Lord, deliver my children from every maternal and paternal generational negative flow of violent nature in Jesus name.

5. Psalms 108:12 KJV, "Give us help from trouble: for vain is the help of man".

O Lord, give my children help from trouble that has been caused by domestic abuse.

6. Colossians 2:14 KJV, "Blotting out the handwriting of ordinances that was against us, which was contrary to us, and took it out of the way, nailing it to his cross".

   Every expected psychological, behavioural, and academic problem associated with domestic violence is cancelled by the blood of Jesus over my children's lives in Jesus name.

7. Isaiah 54:17 KJV, "No weapon that is formed against thee shall prosper; and every tongue that shall rise against thee in judgment thou shalt condemn. This is the heritage of the servants of the Lord, and their righteousness is of me, saith the Lord".

   Every weapon the enemy is fashioning in any form to destroy my children's destiny, it shall not prosper in Jesus name.

   O Lord, heal my children of every visible and invisible damage that has been caused by toxic effects of domestic violence in their lives in Jesus name.

Prayers For The Victim Of Domestic Abuse. (Spouse)

1. Psalms 72:14 KJV, "He shall redeem their soul from deceit and violence: and precious shall their blood be in his sight".

    O Lord, deliver me from being a victim of violence. Don't allow my blood to be shed as a result of domestic abuse. Make my blood precious in your sight.

2. Romans 12:17-18 KJV, "Recompense to no man evil for evil. Provide things honest in the sight of all men. If it be possible, as much as lieth in you, live peaceably with all men".

    O Lord, I receive the grace to live at peace with my spouse and children, irrespective of situation and circumstances in Jesus name. I will not live in unforgiveness, bitterness and vengeance in Jesus name.

3. Psalms 147:3 KJV, "He healeth the broken in heart, and bindeth up their wounds".

    O Lord, heal me of every damage that has been caused in my life as a result of domestic violence in Jesus name.

4. Nahum 1:9 KJV, "What do ye imagine against the Lord? He will make an utter end: affliction shall not rise up the second time".

    The last time I was abused shall be the last in Jesus name. Affliction of domestic violence shall not rise up in my home any longer in Jesus name.

5. James 1:5 KJV, "If any of you lack wisdom, let him ask of God, that giveth to all men liberally, and upbraideth not; and it shall be given him".

    O Lord, give me the wisdom to deal with the root of my spouse's abusive behaviour in Jesus name.

6. Daniel 2:22 KJV, "He revealeth the deep and secret things: he knoweth what is in the darkness, and the light dwelleth with him".

    O Lord, reveal the root of my spouse's abusive behaviour to both of us in Jesus name.

7. Isaiah 49:24-25 KJV, "Shall the prey be taken from the mighty, or the captive delivered? But thus saith the Lord, Even the captives of the mighty shall be taken away, and the prey of the terrible shall be delivered: for I will contend with him that contendeth with thee, and lawful I will save thy children".

    O Lord, according to your word which says the captive of the mighty shall be delivered, deliver my spouse from the stronghold of this violent nature in Jesus name.

About the Author

Oluwatoyin Babatunde is an associate Pastor at Victory International Church, North London, where her husband is the Residence Pastor. She holds a BSC in Midwifery from City University, London and is also a trained nurse.

Toyin, as she is called, is a marriage counsellor who is very passionate about marriage. She is also an anointed speaker at various family and marriage seminars as well as an evangelist and intercessor. She has written numerous literature about marriage along with other edifying write ups. She has a regular teaching called 'The mind of God' which is published on Facebook. The subjects range from marriage to other topics which help with spiritual growth. In conjunction with her husband, she broadcasts a fortnightly marital programme on social media, called 'Marital Matters'.

Pastor Oluwatoyin Babatunde is also a role model teacher on marital issues under the ministry of Domint Institute for Pnemapreneurship Studies, UK. She is also a Sunday school teacher at Victory International Church and Women's leader as a Pastor's wife in the same Ministry.

She is married to Pastor Michael Babatunde who is also an author and great teacher of the word. She mothers three wonderful children, Esther, Oluwafisayomi and Samuel in addition to many spiritual children.

References:

The impact of domestic violence on individuals -

Jill Astbury, Judy Atkinson, Janet E Duke, Patricia L Easteal, Susan E Kurrle, Paul R Tait and Jane Turner

Med J Aust 2000; 173 (8): 427-431. Published online: 16 October 2000

Worship with us at

VICTORY INTERNATIONAL CHURCH
OVERCOMERS PARISH

CHURCH ADRESS: 77 Coburg Road, Wood Green, London, N22 6UB

TELEPHONE: 02086171715, 07043624423, 07908777935

E-MAIL ADDRESS: Info@vicintchurch.co.uk

TIMES OF WORSHIP:

SUNDAYS: 10:00-12:00

TUESDAYS: 19:00-20:00 BIBLE STUDY

THURSDAYS: 19:00-20:00 FASTING AND PRAYER

FACEBOOK PROGRAMME: MARITAL MATTERS @ Oluwatoyin Babatunde or Michael Babatunde